Published by Bloomsbury, New York and London
Distributed to the trade by Holtzbrinck Publishers
Library of Congress Cataloging-in-Publication Data
available upon request.

ISBN 1-58234-934-7

First U.S. Edition

1 3 5 7 9 10 8 6 4 2

Bloomsbury USA Children's Books
175 Fifth Avenue
New York, New York 10010

All papers used by Bloomsbury Publishing are natural, recyclable products made
from wood grown in sustainable, well-managed forests.
The manufacturing processes conform to the environmental regulations of the country of origin.

Grandpa's Surprise

Rosalind Beardshaw

BLOOMSBURY CHILDREN'S BOOKS

Grandpa and Stanley and Bert the dog were looking out of the window when Jack whizzed past on his new tricycle.

They went outside to watch Jack.
“Ooh,” said Stanley, “I like your new tricycle. Can I try it please?”

"I'll think
about it,"
said Jack.

Jack cycled up and down the path. Grandpa and Stanley and Bert waited.

"I've thought about it," said Jack.

"Yes?" said Stanley.

"No!" said Jack.

"Come on, Stanley. I know something that will cheer you up. Let's go to the shed," said Grandpa.

Stanley and Grandpa and Bert went to the shed. Grandpa started to rummage around. Stanley was still sulking.

"Perfect," said Grandpa, as he pulled out an old wooden crate.

"What is that for?" asked Stanley.

"You'll see," said Grandpa.

Then Grandpa dragged out Stanley's old stroller.

"Now then, Stanley, help me take the wheels off this," said Grandpa.

"O.K." said Stanley.

"Screw that on nice and tight," said Grandpa.

"There!" said Stanley.

1

“Finishing touches,” said Grandpa.

“It looks perfect,” said Stanley.

"In we get, Stanley. We'll wear these just in case!" said Grandpa.
"Wheeeee!" shrieked Stanley.

Jack came over to them.

"Do you want a turn on my tricycle now, Stanley?" asked Jack.

"I'll think about it!" said Stanley,
and off they went.

When they came back, Stanley said, "I've thought about it."

"Yes?" said Jack.

“No!” said Stanley.

“Oh,” said Jack.

“But you can come on
the go-kart with us!”
said Stanley.

“HOORAY!”

parp
parp